Little Lessons of Love

In for a penny, in for a pound,
it's love that makes the world go round.

A rolling stone gathers no mate.

Absence makes the heart to wander.

A bird in the hand is worth two in the bush.

Silence is sometimes golden.

He who has no doubts has no sense.

A fool and his partner are soon parted.

Ask me no questions and I'll tell you no lies.

Bad news travels by the classifieds.

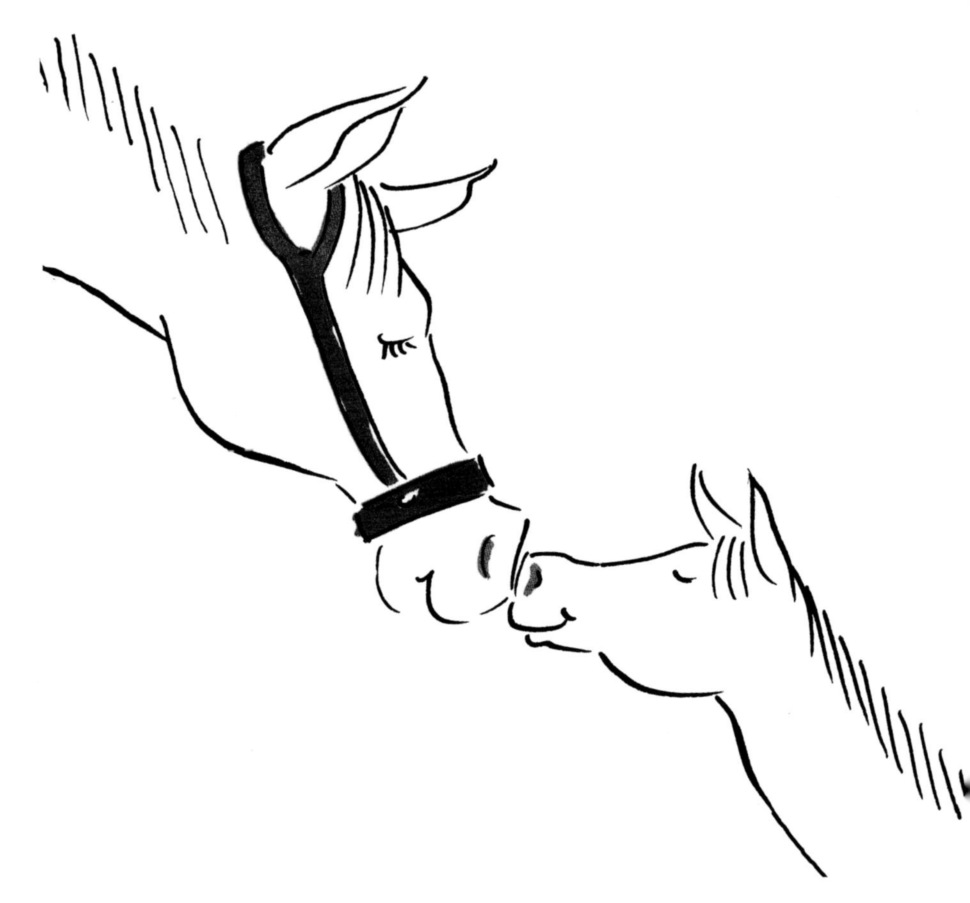

There are none so blind as those in love.

It's no use crying over spoiled milk.

It's easier to catch a little fish from a little pond
than to catch a big fish from a big pond.

After a storm comes the calm.

Great minds think alike;
great couples often diverge.

As you sow, so shall you reap.

As you make your bed, so you must lie in it.

A couple is no stronger than its weakest link.

All that glitters is
not a gold band.

The best of friends may part.

Some roads lead to roam.

No water, no waves.

Actions speak louder than words.

Honesty is not always the best policy.

A friend in need is a friend indeed.

If at first you don't succeed,
ask for her number again.

Ignorance is bliss. (Oh, yeah?)

Something is better than nothing...
except when nothing is better than something.

Massage my back and I'll massage yours.

He who hesitates is lost . . . and alone.

Strike while the iron is hot.

A garlic a day keeps the lover away.

It's best to be on the safe side.

The early bird catches the worm...
but who wants a worm?

It never rains... it pours.

The way to a man's heart is
through white chocolate mousse.

A woman's place is in the Oval Office.

Two's company; three's a triangle.

All work and no play
makes Jack a dull boyfriend.

All is fair in love and war.

The best things in life are hard work.

Better late than pregnant.

All's well that ends well.

Text copyright © 2003 by Blue Apple Books
Illustrations copyright © 2003 by Chris Demarest
All rights reserved
CIP Data is available.
Published in the United States 2003 by
Blue Apple Books
515 Valley Street, Maplewood, N.J. 07040
www.blueapplebooks.com

Distributed in the U.S. by Chronicle Books

First Edition
Printed in China
ISBN 1-59354-018-3
1 3 5 7 9 10 8 6 4 2

Other titles in this series:

Little Lessons from 1st Graders

Little Lessons from Mom

Little Lessons from Dad